D1105649

Rascal Makes Mischief
ON MACKINAC ISLAND

by Cynthia Furlong Reynolds

illustrated by Darrin Brege

mitten press

Text Copyright © 2006 Cynthia Furlong Reynolds
Illustrations Copyright © 2006 Darrin Brege

All rights reserved. No part of this book may be reproduced in any manner
without the express written consent of the publisher, except in the case of
brief excerpts in critical reviews or articles.

All inquiries should be addressed to:
Mitten Press
An imprint of Ann Arbor Media Group LLC
2500 S. State Street
Ann Arbor, MI 48104

Printed and bound in Canada.

10 9 8 7 6 5 4 3 2 1

Library of Congress Cataloging-in-Publication Data

Reynolds, Cynthia Furlong.
  Rascal makes mischief on Mackinac Island / by Cynthia Furlong Reynolds ;
illustrated by Darrin Brege.
       p. cm.
  Summary: During a family vacation, curious young Ben and his mischievous
dog Rascal explore the historic places on Mackinac Island, Michigan, and the
place may never be the same.
  ISBN-13: 978-1-58726-312-5 (hardcover : alk. paper)
  ISBN-10: 1-58726-312-2 (hardcover : alk. paper)
 1. Mackinac Island (Mich.)--Juvenile fiction. [1. Mackinac Island (Mich.)-
-Fiction. 2. Vacations--Fiction. 3. Dogs--Fiction.] I. Brege, Darrin, ill. II.
Title.
 PZ7.R3352Ras 2006
 [E]--dc22
                                    2005036823

This is our dog.

Me and my big brother Charlie found our puppy at a place for lost and lonely pets. We named him Rascal. Dad and Mom mostly call him Rascal-Oh-No! Strangers usually call him Down-Dog-Down!

But everyone calls me Ben.

One of the best things about Rascal is that he loves to take trips. Right now we're on our way to an island called Mackinac, which floats in Lake Huron beside the tippy-top of Michigan's mitten.

Dad says this island is so old that it doesn't even have cars. We'll ride in our car until we get to water and then ride on a boat!

Rascal is very helpful in the car. He hops from side to side, barking to tell Dad the right way to go.

He pants real hard and steams up our windows, so Charlie and me can draw pictures.

He finds all the treats Mom has hidden and opens the bags for us with his teeth. He chews our good dress shoes, so me and Charlie will get to wear our old sneakers to dinner in fancy restaurants.

Finally, just when Rascal's getting tired of making me ask, "Are we there yet?" our car finds Mackinaw City and stops near the water. Dad puts the leash on Rascal so everyone can unload the car.

Rascal loves the boat ride. Above the barking, we can hear someone tell us, "Mackinac is a turtle-shaped island with a rich history and legends that date back to Woodland Indians a thousand years ago... "

Rascal helps the captain by running from side to side on the top deck, warning the seagulls and lighthouses not to hit our boat.

"I hope that your stay on Mackinac is long, sir. You might consider trying one of our competitors' ferries on your return journey," the captain says at the dock. Dad wipes his forehead.

The hotel man loads our suitcases on a cart. We get to ride our bikes and Rascal runs along beside us. We stop to look around on our way to the hotel.

"Wow! I've never seen so many candy stores!" I yell.

Rascal is very happy about that. On the way to our hotel, Rascal licks three little kids' ice-cream cones. He eats a Mackinac cherry-chocolate cone that dropped on the sidewalk and gobbles down an almost-whole foot-long hot dog with chili and mustard and relish and onions. Then he jumps up and grabs a box of fudge from a bike basket.

Rascal doesn't look so good when we get to the hotel. He throws up. Dad tells me to take Rascal far away from the hotel's front door.

Dad decides it's time for our carriage ride. The ride is really, really fun! Rascal makes friends with Warrior and Flash, two very big—make that HUGENORMOUS—horses that are pulling our carriage. Rascal thinks they're big dogs. They think Rascal's a little pest.

"The candy stores on Mackinac Island make 10,000 pounds of fudge every day in the summer," the carriage driver tells us when we start our trip.

Rascal knows what Warrior and Flash are making—and it isn't fudge! It looks like 10,000 pounds of ... well, Mom won't let me say the word!! The driver says that Mackinac horses have their own wagons and clean-up crews. Mom says she wishes Rascal and me had our own clean-up crew.

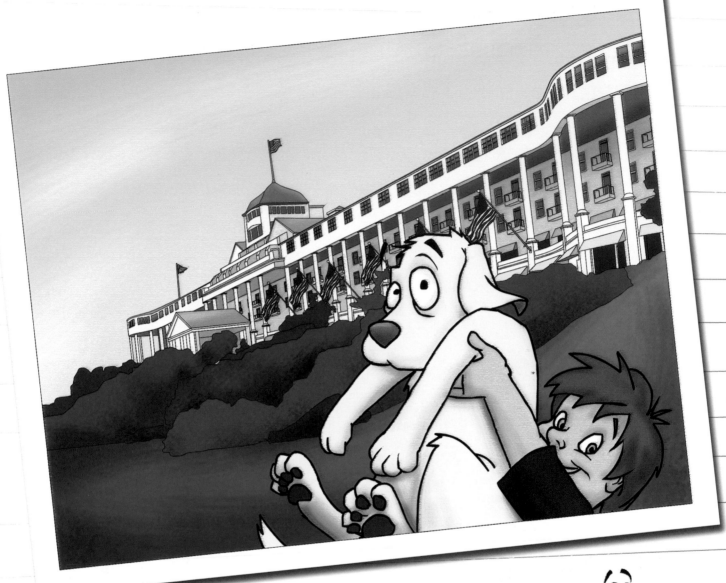

Our first stop is near the great big white fancy Grand Hotel. "A famous movie was filmed at this hotel and it has the longest porch in the world—660 feet," the driver says.

"Great for sliding!" Rascal tells me.

"NOT for sliding!" a man in a uniform tells Rascal after he picks up a lady in a flowery dress. Then me. Then the tray and glasses he accidentally spilled.

"That beautiful big house flying the Michigan flag on the cliff belongs to our Governor," the driver says after we all get in the carriage again.

"Gee, Mom, should we go say hi?" I ask.

Mom shuts her eyes. "I don't think the Governor is ready for us," she says.

Next, a bigger carriage takes us to
a very old Post Cemetery and on
to Skull Cave. The driver tells us
that Indians once hid a friend
there during a battle and the
cave was filled with old bones.
When no one is looking, Rascal
decides to run and peek in the
cave. Rascal would like those
old bones a lot. But the cave
is empty.

Shucks!

Rascal is really, really
disappointed. But I find
our way back to the road
no problem. The carriage
driver seems a little grouchy
when she comes back for us.
I guess the weather's too hot
for her.

The Arch is a stone bridge that reaches 146 feet above water—that's a long way up! Rascal decides it's a great place to play I Spy. Just as we start to crawl toward the top of the bridge, the park ranger grabs me by my shorts and Rascal by his leash and says, "That isn't a good idea, son."

"It was my dog's idea, sir," I say.

The carriage ride ends at the bestest-of-all places: the fort!

Property of
St. Jude Library
South Bend, IN.

The fort is really great! High on a mountain watching the water, it has creepy old buildings and cannons and pretend soldiers with real guns. In the afternoon, the soldiers line up to tell stories and show how people fighted in the old-fashioned days, almost 200 years ago. After they tell us that English soldiers sneaked up on the Americans and won the fort, the pretend soldiers line up, load their guns, and...FIRE!

Rascal gets so excited! He wants to see the guns up close. He jumps on the first soldier, who falls and knocks down the whole line of men. Just like dominos!

When we've run all around the fort, we see grown-ups riding carriages to a big hotel with a big green lawn that has white chairs in lines and a big white tent that doesn't look very good for camping. When Rascal sees a squirrel on a white arch over the bride-lady and a man in a penguin suit, he knows that pets are invited to the wedding, so he runs over to play.

The squirrel jumps down and races Rascal to the big, beautiful cake.

"This is a wedding no one will ever forget," the minister tells my Dad afterward. He and Dad wipe their foreheads. Dad keeps saying he's really, really sorry.

On the way back to our hotel, Rascal has another good idea! Charlie, Rascal, and me splash into the icy cold Lake Huron so we can wash off the delicious white frosting we didn't eat.

Then Rascal gets to shake and chase birds and bark at the boats. Charlie gets to build a sand fort.

I get to JUST SIT STILL AND BE QUIET.

Later, I put on my PJs and brush every one of my teeth and Dad gives me a piggyback ride and Mom kisses me good night and says, "Sleep tight! Don't let the bed bugs bite!" Then I ask, "Dad, can Rascal and me play Sneaky Pete tonight at midnight and find a ghost?"

"Don't even joke about it, son," he says with a little groan as he flicks off the light.

Only guess what?
I'm not joking!

"Good night, everybody!" I yell. "We're having a really, really great adventure, aren't we?" Everybody is very, very quiet.

I lean under the bed to show Rascal my glow-in-the-dark watch with the number 12.

"Wonder where we'll go on vacation next time, Rascal?"